Hey, kids!
See if you can spot Santa,
Mrs. Claus, and Reindeer
hidden throughout the story.

To...
You made it onto Santa's NICE list—GOOD JOB!

MERRY CHRISTMAS!
....

Love, from..

I SAW SANTA

Written by J.D. Green

Illustrated by Nadja Sarell and Srimalie Bassani

sourcebooks
jabberwocky

Santa's not had a vacation all year.
Mrs. Claus says, "Now is a great time, my dear.
I think we should head to our favorite place,
but remember, the children should not see your face!"

"Oh, yes," Santa says, "we should go and pack now!
It's the best place to be, and the food is just…WOW!"

Mrs. Claus says, "Okay, we can set off tonight,
but you heard what I said? You must keep out of sight!"

They load up the sleigh, getting set to explore.
They'll sunbathe, they'll sightsee, they'll shop, and much more!
They leave the North Pole, and all of that snow.
"I won't miss the cold!" Santa says. "Ho! Ho! Ho!"

THE
CANYONS

It's a family tradition, when they go away,
to buy a few gifts to remember their stay.

Smart Mrs. Claus came prepared with a list,
so first she'll go shop—not one friend will be missed!

Santa thinks buying nice gifts is quite tough.
He's feeling confused—there's just so much stuff!

His basket fills up with goodies galore,
such as meatloaf, pecan pie, pizza, and more.

Reindeer's not eager to stick to plans,
there's so much to see and experience firsthand!

But first he must find a good new disguise,
so he can blend in with the crowd outside!

The Clauses are done with their shopping for friends.
Now it's time to go sightseeing before their trip ends!

Back in the North Pole, Head Elf checks the mail.
He opens one letter and turns very pale…

Dear Santa,

I know it's not Christmas, but I wanted
to write and say that I saw someone who
looked just like you! He had a big, white
beard and was hiding in a space rocket
at the museum, eating ice cream!
How funny is that?

Love, your biggest fan!

FREEZE-DRIED
ASTRONAUT ICE CREAM

EXIT

Santa should really be taking more care.
There's one kid who's spotting him everywhere!

Dear Santa,

My mom doesn't believe me, but I really think I saw you today. You were walking through the National Park, wearing green hiking boots and a red-and-white striped backpack, whistling "Jingle Bells". I mean, who sings "Jingle Bells" in the summer? Please tell me it was you?

Love and hugs, your biggest fan!

NATIONAL PARK

Reading the mail, Head Elf shakes his head.
This letter has caused him to turn slightly red!

Hey Santa,

It's me again! On a school trip to the public
library, my friend Ben and I think we saw
you sitting on a bench, wearing sunglasses
and drinking a milkshake. I hope you're
having fun here...?

Love, your biggest fan!

In the North, Head Elf can't believe what he's seeing!
There's one kid who constantly sees Santa fleeing!

Hello Santa,

Okay, so now I'm sure I saw you riding a horse at the fair today. At one point you shouted "Giddy up, Snowball... um... I mean Buttercup." I've also been wondering why you haven't replied to any of my other letters yet? It's almost as if you're not at home to receive them! LOL!

Love, your biggest fan!

Hi Santa,

It IS you that I've been seeing, isn't it?

We were watching the ducks at City Park today when we saw you standing next to a big, red sleigh. No one else owns their own sleigh!

Don't worry, I won't tell anyone, but I would love to know for sure. Please, please write back and tell me if I am right?

All my love, your biggest fan!

The vacation is over, the shopping is done.
It's time to head home. It has been so much fun!

When they arrive home, Head Elf lets Santa know
he was spotted at every location. Oh no!

He reads through the letters, and what does he spot?
"They're ALL from one child!" he exclaims. "The whole lot!"

So Santa thinks hard, then he knows what to do...
He sits down and writes something special, to YOU!

To my biggest fan,

Hello, Santa here. It WAS me in each place!
Each letter you wrote put a smile on my face.

When you are around it is no good me hiding.
You spotted me swimming, and eating, and riding!

Please keep this a secret, so this time next year
we can all return and enjoy our time here!

There's so much to see and there's so much to do.
Perhaps next vacation we can come stay with you?

Merry Christmas!

Love, Santa

X

Written by J.D. Green
Illustrated by Nadja Sarell and Srimalie Bassani
Additional art by Darran Holmes
Designed by Geff Newland

Published by Sourcebooks Jabberwocky, an imprint of Sourcebooks, Inc.
P.O. Box 4410, Naperville, Illinois 60567-4410
(630) 961-3900
Fax: (630) 961-2168
jabberwockykids.com

Date of Production: August 2018
Run Number: HTW_PO201802
Printed and bound in China (GD)
10 9 8 7 6 5 4 3 2 1